You can be a
Brownie Girl Scout, too!

If you are 6, 7, or 8 years old, or in the 1st, 2nd, or 3rd grade, just ask your parents to look in your local telephone directory under "Girl Scouts," and call for information. You can also ask your parents to call **Girl Scouts of the U.S.A.** at **1-(212) 852-8000** or write to 420 Fifth Avenue, New York, NY 10018-2702 to find out about becoming a Girl Scout in your area.

For Juliana — J.O'C.

To my grandparents — L.S.L.

Copyright © 1993 by Girl Scouts of the United States of America. All rights reserved. Published by Grosset & Dunlap, Inc., a member of The Putnam & Grosset Group, New York, in cooperation with Girl Scouts of the United States of America. GROSSET & DUNLAP is a trademark of Grosset & Dunlap, Inc. Published simultaneously in Canada. Printed in the U.S.A.

Library of Congress Cataloging-in-Publication Data
O'Connor, Jane.
    Sarah's incredible idea / by Jane O'Connor ; illustrated by Laurie Struck Long.
        p.   cm.—(Here come the Brownies)
    Summary: Shy Sarah has a great idea for her Brownie Girl Scout troop but is not sure she is brave enough to speak up.
    [1. Girl Scouts—Fiction.   2. Courage—Fiction.]   I. Long, Laurie Struck, ill.
II. Title. III. Series.
PZ7.O222Sar   1993
[E]—dc20   92-36803
    ISBN 0-448-40162-2 (pbk.)   E F G H I J
    ISBN 0-448-40163-0 (GB)   A B C D E F G H I J

HERE COME THE BROWNIES
A Brownie Girl Scout Book

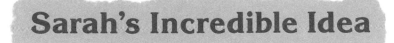

Sarah's Incredible Idea

By Jane O'Connor
Illustrated by Laurie Struck Long

Grosset & Dunlap • New York
In association with GIRL SCOUTS OF THE U.S.A.

1

It was snack time at the Friday Brownie Girl Scout troop meeting. Carrot sticks and goldfish crackers.

The troop always met in the school lunchroom. And the heavy smell of today's lamb stew still hung in the air. The idea of eating lambs, cute cuddly lambs, made Sarah's tummy do a flip-flop. She loved animals. All kinds. In fact, she often thought she understood animals better than she understood people.

"My aunt is coming to school again," Marsha was telling the troop. "She came to my class last year. She brought a real dinosaur bone that she found. That's her job. She finds fossils. The bone was zillions of years old."

"I remember that," Sarah said. "I thought it sounded so fun to be a dinosaur hunter."

Marsha turned to Sarah. "Oh! Were you in my class last year? I forgot."

Marsha did not say it in a mean way at all. Still, Sarah felt like shouting, "Yes. I was in your class last year. And we were in kindergarten together, too. But you probably don't remember that either."

Instead, Sarah bit down on a carrot stick. Here she was. The second tallest kid in the second grade. So how come nobody ever seemed to notice her? In school pictures she was always in the back row. In their class play, "The Wizard of Oz," Sarah got the part of a tree.

"Watch this!" Amy threw three goldfish crackers high up in the air. Then—one, two, three—she caught them in her mouth.

"No applause, please," said Amy. She held out her arm as if she had to keep all her fans away from her.

Sarah sighed. She wished she were more like Amy. Amy was always doing funny stuff. Amy could talk like Donald Duck. Amy could crack her knuckles really loudly. Amy was not a back row person at all.

"Now that you've all had a chance to chow down," said their troop leader, "guess what I brought with me." Their troop leader's name was Mrs. Quinones. But everybody called her Mrs. Q.

Today Mrs. Q. had a large yellow gym bag with her. It was zipped up so nobody could tell what was inside.

"Is it dress-up clothes?" asked Krissy A.

Mrs. Q. shook her head.

"I know! I know!" said Amy. "It's a sleeping bag."

"No." Mrs. Q. smiled. "I know I told you we're going to learn how to roll up a sleeping bag before we go on our overnight. But that's not what I have in here. Guess again. It's something you all asked me to bring a couple of meetings ago."

Sarah thought hard. Their troop was going to go ice-skating once it got cold. But why would Mrs. Q. bring in ice skates now? Then Sarah remembered something else. Mrs. Q. had told the girls that her cousin was a pilot. Her pilot cousin was going to send Mrs. Q. an old parachute. Sarah peered at the bag. Yes! She bet that's exactly what it was. The parachute!

Sarah wanted to shout out her guess. But what if she wasn't right? Sarah's face always got so red whenever she got stuff wrong in class. Maybe that would happen here too, at the Brownie meeting.

"It's the parachute!" said Corrie.

"Bingo!" said Mrs. Q. as she unzipped the yellow bag.

I *knew* it was the parachute! I should have said something, Sarah told herself as Corrie got up to help Mrs. Q. take the parachute out of the bag.

"Oooh! I didn't think it would be so pretty!" said Corrie.

The parachute *was* pretty. It had big stripes in all different colors. When it was

all spread out, it looked like a giant
rainbow. Mrs. Q. asked each girl to hold
onto part of the edge. Then she showed the
girls how to make little waves with the
parachute. Sarah liked the way the
parachute rippled and billowed over their
heads.

As they made bigger and bigger waves,
the parachute began to buck and flap. It
made funny, loud flapping noises.

"It sounds like the parachute is burping!" said Amy. "And it didn't even say excuse me. Some manners!"

The Brownies laughed. So did Mrs. Q. Then she showed the girls lots of games they could play with the parachute. The girls picked up the parachute, threw it up in the air, and let it float down on top of them. Everyone loved that. They did it again and again. Sometimes two girls from opposite sides ran under and switched places. Sarah liked that best of all.

Sarah was sorry when Mrs. Q. said it was almost time to pack up the parachute.

"We can play just one more game," Mrs. Q. told the girls. "This is a thinking game. Who would like to be It?"

Several hands shot up. But Sarah kept hers down.

"Okay... Krissy S. You can be It."

Krissy S. jumped up.

"Please, go outside in the hallway," Mrs. Q. told Krissy S. "Wait there until I say to come back. One Brownie will be hiding under the parachute. It will be up to you to figure out who it is."

While Krissy S. waited outside, Mrs. Q. looked around the circle. "Let's see," Mrs. Q. said slowly. "Who shall I pick to hide?"

"ME! ME! ME!" lots of girls shouted.

Mrs. Q. placed a finger over her lips. "Krissy will hear you!" Mrs. Q.'s eyes travelled from girl to girl. "Okay. You are It."

Mrs. Q. was pointing straight at Sarah. Sarah crawled under the parachute.

Sarah was never too crazy about being It in games like Tag or Monkey in the Middle. But now all she had to do was hide. Why, anybody could do that.

"I hope it's not too hot under there," Mrs. Q. said.

"No. It's fine," Sarah told her. In fact, it was kind of cozy inside. Sarah felt like a bear in a cave, snuggling down for winter.

From the other side of the parachute, Sarah could hear Mrs. Q. calling for Krissy S. to come back. Lots of Brownies were giggling. Mrs. Q. had to keep reminding them not to say a word.

"So, Krissy, who is our mystery Brownie?"

"Hmmmm. Well, it's not Amy. Or Marsha. Or Lauren. 'Cause I see them," Sarah heard Krissy S. say. "And it's not Jo

Ann. Or Corrie or Krissy A. I see them too. Hmmmm. Who could it be?"

Several girls were giggling again.

"Remember. No clues!" said Mrs. Q.

"Is it Sharnelle?" asked Krissy S.

"No. Sharnelle is not here today," said Mrs. Q. "Take a good look around. Try and think of everybody in the troop." Then Mrs. Q. lifted up a little piece of the parachute. She winked at Sarah. "Yes. She's still under there."

Sarah smiled back. But she was starting to get a funny feeling in her tummy. She didn't like being under the parachute anymore. She felt hot now. And uncomfortable. "It's me under here!" she wanted to shout out. "ME! SARAH!"

"So? Who is it?" Mrs. Q. asked Krissy S. once again.

But after a few more seconds, all Krissy S. said was, "Gee. This is too hard. I give up."

"All right then. Our mystery girl may come out now. Show Krissy S. who you are."

Sarah crawled out from under the parachute. All four feet, nine inches of her. "Surprise. It's me," she said in a small voice.

"Sarah!" Krissy S. really did look surprised to see her. "Dumb me!" Krissy S. smacked herself on the forehead.

"Invisible me," thought Sarah, while she and the other girls helped Mrs. Q. fold up the parachute.

2

The meeting soon came to an end. Some parents were already waiting by the door of the lunchroom. There was time for just one song. So all the Brownie Girl Scouts held hands in a circle and sang,

> "Make new friends
> But keep the old.
> One is silver
> But the other's gold."

It was Sarah's favorite song. Sarah loved the way they sang it in rounds with everybody starting at a different time. But today Sarah hardly heard the music.

The whole time Sarah kept thinking that it wouldn't matter if she never came to another meeting. Nobody would miss her. Oh, maybe after about a year somebody would say, "I wonder whatever happened to that tall kid. The one with the big front teeth."

Sarah's mood was no better by the time she got home. In fact, she felt worse. Every time she turned the corner onto her street, she still expected to see her friend Mr. Feldman. He had lived in the condo next to hers. And he always used to be outside gardening. He was such a nice man. Why, he didn't even get mad the time Sarah's puppy dug up his flowers. But Mr. Feldman did not live in Shady Acres anymore. He had to move to a nursing home last month, after he broke his hip.

All the condos in Shady Acres looked exactly the same. Mr. Feldman's had stood out because of all the flowers. There had been flower boxes at every window...rosebushes on either side of the front door... and a wooden goose stuck in the grass. Now the goose was gone. In its place was a sign that said, "For Sale."

"I miss Mr. Feldman," Sarah said to her mom as they came up their front walk. She thought about the Brownie song they had sung. Mr. Feldman was a gold friend.

"I miss him, too," said her mom.

"The first time I met Mr. Feldman, he told me he would never forget my name.

That was because his wife's name had been Sarah too. And he never did forget my name either."

"Why don't you give him a call?" Sarah's mom suggested. She was fishing around in her bag for her keys.

Sarah bit her lip. "Um. I don't know." Sarah felt funny calling Mr. Feldman. Mr. Feldman was easy to talk to. But she'd never spoken to him on the telephone. She never had to. Mr. Feldman was just always outside weeding and planting while Sarah was outside playing with her puppy, Muffin. Mr. Feldman always saved big fat worms and slugs in a pot of dirt for Sarah. He knew she liked looking at that kind of stuff. And he always had two big raisin bagels wrapped in a paper napkin. One was for Sarah. One for Muffin.

"I bet he'd love to hear from you," Sarah's mom said.

"I know," said Sarah. "But what would I say to him? 'Hello, Mr. Feldman. How is your nursing home?' That would sound so dumb."

Sarah and her mom opened their front door. Muffin was right on the other side, waiting for Sarah. In a flash, she was all over Sarah.

"Hey. Somebody missed me. Didn't you, girl? Didn't you?" Sarah buried her nose in Muffin's soft fur.

Muffin wagged her tail wildly and kissed Sarah, who did not mind getting dog slobber all over her face. It was nice knowing somebody missed her.

That made Sarah think about Mr. Feldman again. She sure missed him. But how did he know that? Okay. She would call him. After all, Sarah was a Brownie Girl Scout. And being a Brownie Girl Scout meant doing nice things for other people. Even if it was a little hard.

Right after Sarah took Muffin for a walk, she had her mother look up the number of the Star of David Home for the Aged.

Sarah dialed the number.

"I'd like Mr. Sam Feldman's room, please," Sarah said.

"Hello? Hello? Who is it?" Mr. Feldman said in a loud voice a second later. "Who's there?"

"It's me, Mr. Feldman. Sarah."

"Who? Sherry? I don't know any Sherry."

"IT'S SARAH, Mr. Feldman." Sarah shouted her name this time.

"Oh, Sarah!" Mr. Feldman laughed.

"You know me. I don't hear so well. Sarah! Imagine that! You calling me!"

The phone call did not last long. Sarah told Mr. Feldman that Muffin was still chewing up stuff that she shouldn't. Like her father's bathrobe. Lucky for Sarah that her dad was a vet and understood about puppies.

Then she told Mr. Feldman that her mother bought the same raisin bagels for her and Muffin. But they didn't taste the same.

"Tell her to wrap them in a paper napkin. That's the secret!" said Mr. Feldman.

Sarah and Mr. Feldman both laughed. Then Mr. Feldman said to give Muffin a hug for him and they said good-by.

Sarah was happy she had called Mr. Feldman. But she felt sad, too. She went up to her room with Muffin trotting behind.

While Muffin curled up for a nap, Sarah fed her fish. She changed Norma's kitty litter. And she played with her hamsters, Huey, Dewey, and Louie.

Sarah loved all kinds of animals. Even slugs and worms and roaches. They were alive just like her, after all. Mr. Feldman understood. He felt the same way about plants and flowers. "We're all God's creatures," he used to say.

"Can you visit people in a nursing home?" Sarah asked her parents at dinner that night. "'Cause I would like to see Mr. Feldman." Sarah had not realized she wanted to. Not until she said it.

"What a sweet idea!" Sarah's mom leaned over and kissed Sarah. "You are such a nice girl. Nice through and through. Do you want to see if we can go tomorrow?"

Sarah shook her head no. Saturday was her day to help out her dad at the animal clinic. When she grew up, Sarah was going to be a vet, just like her dad. "And anyway, it's Shabbat," Sarah explained to her parents. That was Hebrew for "Sabbath." "It's Mr. Feldman's day to pray. But Sunday afternoon would be okay."

So Sarah's mom called and found out the visiting hours.

Sarah tugged at her mother's arm while she was on the phone. "Ask if you can bring pets too."

Sarah's mom shook her head. "Oh, no, sweetie. I don't think that would be such a good idea."

"Come on. Just ask."

"You don't allow dogs to visit, do you?" Sarah's mom paused. "Oh! You do? As long as they're healthy and friendly."

"Yippee!" yelled Sarah. Muffin was going with her!

3

On Sunday Sarah gave Muffin a bath. She used up lots of Pretty Puppy shampoo. Muffin smelled almost as good as Mr. Feldman's rosebushes.

Then Sarah put on her tee shirt that said, "Save the Whales" and the polka-dot leggings her grandma had sent for her birthday. Today she wanted to look extra special.

Now she and Muffin were both ready.

Sarah's dad drove her over to the Star of David Home for the Aged. It looked just like a regular apartment building from the outside. But inside it was filled with people Mr. Feldman's age or older. Sarah had never seen so many old people in one place!

In the rec room a lady in a wheelchair was knitting a little sweater. Nearby, four

men sat around a table. They were playing a card game. A few people were reading the Sunday newspaper. A lot more were sitting around snoozing. A giant TV set was turned on with the sound way up high. Still, the whole place seemed quiet. Too quiet.

"We're here to see Mr. Sam Feldman," Sarah's dad told the lady at the front desk.

The lady rang Mr. Feldman's room. "He'll be right down."

Sarah waited by the elevators. Muffin strained on her leash. Again and again the silver doors of the elevator slid open. Each time Sarah expected to see Mr. Feldman.

At last, out he came. He walked slowly. And he had to use a cane. But when he saw Sarah he broke into a big smile.

"Imagine. You coming all the way out to see me." Mr. Feldman shook hands with Sarah's dad. Then he patted Sarah on the cheek. "Come, Sarah. We'll sit. I'm still not so good on my feet. But first I want you to meet a few people."

"So. This is the young Sarah I hear so much about," said the lady who was knitting. Then she turned to Sarah's puppy.

"And this must be Muffin. I've heard about her, too." She tickled Muffin under her chin.

Right away Muffin made a grab for her yarn. "Oh, no, you don't!" the lady laughed. "I am knitting this for a brand-new baby. My great-grandson!"

Sarah met every single person in the rec room. Sarah felt shy. She was not used to having such a fuss made of her.

"So this is your friend, Sam!" said a man near Mr. Feldman.

"No wonder you miss her," said a lady with beautiful, snowy white hair. "What a cute little girl."

Sarah's face turned red. She did not think of herself as cute or little. Most people when they met her said, "My! Aren't you big for your age!"

Muffin was a big hit, too. Everyone wanted to pet her. Muffin loved all the fuss. But she was getting more and more excited.

Before Sarah could stop her, Muffin broke away. In a flash, Muffin was on top of the card table. She had spotted food. And she wanted it!

"Oy! The dog!" one cardplayer shouted.

Cards flew everywhere! The plate of food went sailing across the room like a Frisbee. Then it crashed to the floor.

"I'm so sorry!" Sarah's dad said to the men. He already had Muffin in hand.

But the men didn't seem to mind. They were laughing.

"Stop. Don't be silly," said one man. "We sit here playing cards all day. What's one game less?"

"I had a terrible hand anyway," said another man.

"Look! She still has her eye on the food," said somebody else. "Let her eat. It's just some kosher salami. It couldn't hurt."

Muffin had quite a feast.

"Such a smart dog!" one of the men said.

"And a lovely color, too. I had a dog like that," another man told Sarah. "What a wonderful pet he was."

By the time Sarah was ready to leave, the Star of David nursing home did not seem so quiet. She could hardly hear the TV anymore because so many people were talking.

"Maybe you'll come again," Mr. Feldman said.

"Of course I will," Sarah told him.

"I have a little something for you."

Mr. Feldman handed Sarah a folded-up paper napkin. Sarah knew there would be raisin bagels inside. One for her. One for Muffin.

"Thanks!" said Sarah. She was not a hugging kind of girl. So she waved. And she made Muffin waggle her paw at everybody. Then she and her dad left.

"Well, you sure made everyone's day," her dad said in the car.

"Muffin too," said Sarah. "I bet those people would have more fun if there were some pets at the nursing home."

Muffin was snuggled up beside Sarah. She could feel Muffin's warm breath on her arm. She couldn't imagine not having a dog. It would be so lonesome.

"I know what you mean," her dad answered. "Everybody needs somebody to love and care for. Did you know that people who live alone live longer if they have a pet? But I guess a nursing home has enough to do, caring for so many people. Pets can be quite a big job, you know."

Sarah nodded. She guessed that she understood. But it was still sad.

4

The next week was a busy one. And Sarah did not have much time to think about Mr. Feldman or the Star of David Home for the Aged.

Everyone in 2-B was studying volcanoes. Sarah and Corrie were doing a project together on Mount Vesuvius. Mount Vesuvius was a volcano in Italy that had buried two whole towns when it erupted a long time ago.

Sarah and Corrie were making a papier-mâché volcano of Mount Vesuvius with two miniature towns at the bottom. Sarah was lucky to have Corrie as her partner. Corrie was the best artist in second grade. She had made lots of little houses out of empty matchboxes. She had made trees out of twigs.

Sarah was not so hot at art. But she didn't mind getting her hands gooky. So she mixed all the stuff to make the mountain. She dug out the inside so the mountain was hollow. That was where they were going to pour in some oatmeal "lava." Sarah painted the mountain brown and stuck in the matchbox houses and little twig trees that Corrie had made. She also took some pebbles from her fish tank and made little roads between the matchbox houses.

Sarah and Corrie worked together almost every afternoon after school at Sarah's house. Corrie didn't have any pets of her own. Her mom was allergic. Corrie loved playing with all of Sarah's pets. Louie the hamster most of all. Corrie liked to put Louie on Mount Vesuvius and shout, "Run for your life, Louie. The volcano is about to erupt!"

The last thing Corrie and Sarah did was their report. They had each read two books about the towns that got wiped out by the volcano. Instead of writing out their report, they decided it would be fun to make a tape to play for their class. Sarah was the narrator and told the story of Mount Vesuvius. Corrie played the part of all the scared villagers. They even had sound effects. For the erupting volcano, they recorded rumbling sounds by putting tennis shoes in the dryer. Then, Sarah's dad turned on the vacuum cleaner and held it way up close to the tape recorder. It sounded great.

When Sarah and Corrie handed in their project on Friday, Mrs. Fujikawa clapped her hands in delight.

"This is outstanding!" Mrs. Fujikawa did

not say "outstanding" very often. She saved
"outstanding" for the very, very best work.
"I am so proud of you girls. I can see you
worked very hard."

Mrs. Fujikawa's words made Sarah feel
wonderful. Her teacher set the volcano on
the windowsill for the whole class to see.
All day long kids came up and told her and
Corrie that theirs was the best. Sarah didn't
know what to say. Still, it was nice getting
so much attention. It was nice being
noticed.

Sarah was still thinking about this during
the Brownie Girl Scout meeting after school.

Everybody was sitting cross-legged in a
circle on the floor of the lunchroom. This
was their Brownie Ring. It was where the
girls talked over things that had happened to

each of them. It was also where they planned out stuff they wanted to do as a troop.

Mrs. Q. was talking about that now. "We know that doing nice things for other people is a very important part of being a Brownie Girl Scout."

The girls nodded. Helping others was part of the Girl Scout promise. They all repeated the words to the promise at the start of every meeting.

"So I'd like everybody to think about something our troop can do together. Something that will be fun and will make other people feel happy. Does anyone have an idea?"

The girls all thought for a moment. Then one by one, several hands shot up. Mrs. Q.

wrote down each idea. Soon she had a long list.

1.) MAKING PUPPETS FOR CHILDREN IN THE HOSPITAL.

2.) COLLECTING CANS OF FOOD FOR HUNGRY PEOPLE.

3.) ADOPTING A PARK AND PLANTING NEW TREES.

4.) BECOMING PEN PALS WITH GIRL SCOUTS IN OTHER TROOPS.

"These are all fine ideas," Mrs. Q. said. "Anyone else?"

Sarah looked around the Brownie Girl Scout Ring. She did have another idea. It was a good idea too, she thought . . . but what if nobody else thought so?

Sarah kept her hand down.

5

"I guess we will take a vote then," Mrs. Q. said. She handed the list to Marsha, who read out each idea. The girls raised their hands for the ideas they liked best. It was a close vote. But adopting a park won.

McCormack Park was right across the street from school. Mrs. Q. said she would call the parks department and let the girls know what she found out at their next meeting.

"We adopted a park in my old troop. Before I moved here," Amy told Sarah on their way out. "It was nice. We raked leaves. And planted some new trees. But I wish we could have thought of something more original." Sarah just nodded. She should have raised her hand and told everybody her idea. Why did she always act like such a scaredy-cat?

At dinner that night, Sarah picked at her food. She didn't even tell her parents about the fuss Mrs. Fujikawa made over her volcano. When her parents weren't looking, Sarah slipped half her hamburger to Muffin under the table. That was strictly a no-no.

"You seemed awfully quiet tonight, honey," Sarah's mom said later, while she tucked Sarah into bed. "Are things okay at school?"

Sarah just shrugged. "I'm a quiet child." Wasn't that what all her teachers wrote on every report? *Sarah is a lovely girl, but she needs to learn to speak up more.*

Her mom gave her a hug. "I know you're quiet. I am too. But I can tell the difference between quiet and unhappy."

Sarah let out a gusty sigh. Then she came out with it. "At Brownies today I had a really neat idea for something our whole troop could do together...but I was too chicken to say it. I was scared maybe some kids would think it was dumb. So I just sat there and kept my mouth shut. Like I always do."

Sarah's mom nodded. "I was the same way. I know it's hard sometimes to speak up in front of lots of people—even when they're your friends. But you have so many wonderful ideas. You just have to let other people know about them."

Maybe so, thought Sarah. But this time it was too late. She had missed her chance.

At the next troop meeting, the Brownies talked excitedly about adopting a park.

But Mrs. Q. had some disappointing news.

"McCormack Park has already been adopted," she said. "The Junior Girl Scout troop beat us to it."

When she heard that, Sarah looked up. The park was out. Here was her chance to speak up.

"I saved the list of ideas from last week,"

Mrs. Q went on. "So I guess we'll just take another vote." Mrs. Q. began reading. "Who wants to make puppets for the children's wing at the hospital? Please raise your hands."

Sarah's heart was going thump thump thump. It was now or never. Up went her hand.

Mrs. Q. looked up to count. "Okay, Sarah. That's one vote for puppets."

"Um, no, Mrs. Q. Um, I don't want to make puppets. Well, that's not what I mean." Sarah gulped. She felt like her tongue was twisting itself into a pretzel! "I mean, making puppets is nice...but I have another idea I thought maybe I could suggest." Sarah paused.

Mrs. Q. smiled a smile of encouragement. "Please, Sarah. Go on."

"Well, I went to visit my friend at the Star of David Home for the Aged. His name is Mr. Feldman. He broke his hip. That's why he went to the nursing home. Well, anyway, when I went to visit him, I brought along my puppy, Muffin, too." Sarah paused. Was this starting to sound dumb? She looked around. But nobody was laughing. They were sitting and listening.

So Sarah kept going.

"Well. All the people there are old. They liked seeing a kid like me. And they liked seeing my puppy, too. I thought maybe our whole troop could visit all the people there. And everybody could bring a pet."

There. She had said it.

Right away there was a little buzz of excitement.

"I could bring Skippy. That's my guinea pig," said Amy.

"And my kitten, Snowball, could come. She is very friendly," said Marsha.

"Do you think anybody would mind if I took my garter snake?" asked Lauren.

"Wait! What about me?" Corrie wailed. "I don't have any pets. Not even a crummy goldfish! My mother is allergic to just about everything!"

"That's okay," Sarah told her. "I'll lend you one of mine. I have plenty of pets to go around."

Everybody liked Sarah's idea. They liked it a lot. They didn't even bother to go on with the vote. There was no contest!

6

On Sunday afternoon everybody met in front of school. Sarah was wearing her Brownie Girl Scout uniform. She had put it on her armchair last night. This morning she had woken up to find the bottom part of her sash chewed away. Muffin had struck again. But who cared! Today was going to be a great day.

Everybody piled into a big bus.

Besides the Brownies and some parents, there were five puppies, three kittens, several mice and hamsters, one parrot, one garter snake, and two box turtles going to the Star of David Home for the Aged. Mrs. Q. had checked everything out with the nursing home. Everybody was welcome.

Corrie, who was in charge of Louie the hamster for the day, sat beside Sarah.

"I have a surprise for you. But my lips are sealed," Corrie told Sarah. Then she pretended to zip up her mouth.

The trip was noisy. Very noisy. Dogs barked. Cats meowed. Jo Ann's parrot was squawking its head off. On top of all that, Amy started singing a song. The tune was to "Glory, Glory, Hallelujah." But the words were different.

"I know a song that gets on everybody's nerves," Amy sang. "I know a song that gets on everybody's nerves. I know a song that gets on everybody's nerves. And this is how it gooooooes." Amy paused for a second. Then she started singing the exact same verse all over again. Soon everybody was singing along with her.

"I know a song that gets on everybody's nerves . . ."

Finally Mrs. Q. raised her right hand. It was the Brownie Girl Scout sign for quiet.

"The song works, girls. It certainly is getting on our nerves. All the grown-ups, at least. So let's give it a rest."

Mrs. Q. and the other parents looked thankful when the bus turned into the parking lot of the Star of David Home for the Aged.

There were even more people in the rec room this time. Lots more.

At first all the Brownies were very quiet. Even Amy.

The man who ran the nursing home welcomed everybody. And Mrs. Q. said how happy all the Brownie Girl Scouts were to be their guests. Then Jo Ann's parrot started squawking.

"Where's the chow? Where's the chow?" it screamed over and over.

That was all it took to break the ice.

Soon everyone was chatting.

"Hey. How come you're wearing a beanie?" Amy asked Mr. Feldman. "It kind of looks like my Brownie beanie."

"That's not a beanie," Sarah told Amy. "It's a yarmulke. It's religious. Mr. Feldman wears it for praying."

"Oops!" Amy clapped a hand over her mouth. "Sorry."

"That's all right. Today I'm an honorary Brownie," said Mr. Feldman smiling at Amy.

Sarah noticed that Mr. Feldman was also wearing a clip-on bow tie today. The lady in the wheelchair was all dressed up, too. She waved at Sarah. Then she went back to petting a hamster.

One of the box turtles was missing for a while. And a puppy named Simone got overexcited and threw up.

Still, the visit was a great success.

Only Corrie seemed to be acting strange. She kept turning and looking at the front door.

Then while Mr. Feldman was giving each girl a small pot of violets, Corrie suddenly stood up. She punched the air with her fist.

"Yesssss! She's here!" Corrie shouted.

Sarah turned around. So did everybody else.

Corrie's mom was coming through the front door. A guy with a camera around his neck was with her.

"This is the surprise. The surprise I couldn't tell you about." Corrie was beaming now. "My mom is going to write a newspaper story on us." She turned to Sarah. "On you, really. This whole thing was your idea. Just think. You'll be famous!"

"Famous? Me?" The idea made Sarah nervous and excited at the same time. She took a deep breath. "Oh, well. Here goes!"

Sarah answered Corrie's mom's questions as best she could. Corrie's mom kept on coughing and sneezing. She sure was allergic to pets. The photographer kept snapping pictures. Especially at the end when everybody held hands and sang together.

"Make new friends
But keep the old.
One is silver
But the other's gold."

The song had never sounded sweeter to Sarah. Mr. Feldman squeezed her hand while they sang.

Sure enough, the story appeared in Monday's paper. Along with a big photo of the Brownies, their pets, and their new friends at the Star of David Home for the Aged.

And this time Sarah was not in the back row. Oh, no! She was right in front!

Girl Scout Ways

If you visit a home for the elderly like Sarah's troop did, you'll probably make some new friends. And you can make those friends feel really special by sending them homemade greeting cards. It's a fun activity that you can do at home or at a Brownie Girl Scout troop meeting!

You can make almost any kind of card, but one really neat idea is a puzzle card—a card that the receiver has to put together in order to read the message!

- Here's what you'll need to make a puzzle card: construction paper, cardboard, colored markers, pens, pencils, or crayons, scissors, glue, and an envelope.

- First cut the cardboard and the construction paper to the size you want your puzzle to be. Then glue the two pieces together. Now it's time to design your card and decide on the message you want to send. (You might want to practice this part on a piece of scrap paper.) Use the construction paper side of your card to write your message.

- When you finish your card, turn it over so that the cardboard side is face up. Draw lines that show the pieces of the puzzle. You can have as many pieces as you want—lots if you want the puzzle to be hard or not so many if you want it to be easier. Once you've drawn your lines, you can cut the puzzle apart. (If you need to use sharp scissors, be sure to have a grown-up supervise.)

- Now you can put the puzzle pieces in an envelope. And you're ready to either give your card to someone or send it in the mail. If you do mail it, you can ask a grown-up to help you get the complete address and correct postage on the envelope.